Picnic on a Cloud

Look   Follow David, his huge dog, Newton, and their friend Jessica on an exciting adventure.

Learn   Each project teaches a scientific principle and shares a history lesson with you.

Do   Have fun building your own project with materials found around the house.

Created by Mark Icanberry
Illustrated by Mark Icanberry and Arthur Mount

Look • Learn & Do Publications

LOOK • LEARN & DO SERIES™

Picnic on a Cloud

Picnic on a Cloud © 2000 by Mark Icanberry
Created by Mark Icanberry
Illustrated by Mark Icanberry and Arthur Mount • Layout by Carlton Rémy

I dedicate this book to my son David. Special thanks to my friends and family, and most of all to my wife, Nina, for her incredible support, patience, and love.

ISBN 1-893327-02-7
Printed in Singapore
10 9 8 7 6 5 4 3 2 1

Look • Learn & Do Publications
www.lldkids.com

Distributed by Ten Speed Press, P.O. Box 7123, Berkeley, CA 94707 • www.tenspeed.com

Picnic on a Cloud

David, his huge dog, Newton, and their friend Jessica spend all their free time building things and having adventures with their projects. They are helped by David's father, Professor Alexander. He is a creative inventor who instructs them on the scientific principles and histories of each project they want to build. The adventure of the picnic on a cloud began early one Saturday morning.

Newton slowly opened his large, lazy eyelids. David yawned and called from below, "Are you up yet, Newton?" "Rup," replied Newton. David pulled on his favorite jeans and they headed downstairs for breakfast.

"What do you want to build today, Newton?" asked David after a big gulp of orange juice.

"Ri ron't row," gurgled Newton, slurping up his breakfast.

"So, you're going to Dad's shop today?" asked David's mother.

"Yes," answered David. "We're going to meet Jessica, and then we'll decide what to build."

After helping his mother make their lunch, David and Newton headed out into the warm morning sun.

"Hi, David. Hi, Newton," called Jessica,
skipping up the hill to meet them.

As they crossed the creaky old wooden bridge, the three young adventurers saw a shiny silver blimp flying above.

"That's it! That's it!" cried Jessica.
"Let's build a blimp today."
"Ra ho," barked Newton as they ran
to find Professor Alexander.

Bursting into the professor's huge workshop, which was filled from floor to rafters with all sorts of machines, supplies, and gadgets, David shouted, "Dad! Dad! Where are you? We want to build a blimp today."

Professor Alexander stood up from his work in the loft and looked down. "I'm up here. Come on up, and we'll see what we can do."

"Will you show us how to build a blimp?" asked Jessica.

"Yes, we want to fly," added David.

"Rup!" barked Newton as he scratched one big droopy ear.

"That sounds great! Let's see what we can find in the computer," said Professor Alexander.

The four huddled around the screen, searching for information on building blimps and how to fly them.

With Professor Alexander's help, the adventurers planned how they would build their own airship. The blueprint listed all the supplies they needed, and using it as a guide, they searched all over the workshop to find them.

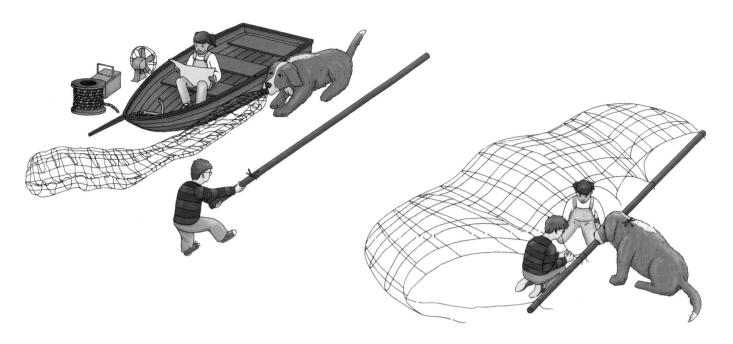

First they carried all the supplies to an open area of the barn where they could construct the airship.

Next they began assembling the pieces. To hold the balloons in place, they tied a net to a long pole.

As Jessica and David worked on assembling the propeller fan, Newton brought in the sandbags to use for weight.

After all the parts of the airship were in place, they worked together to fill the 289 balloons that would lift them high into the air.

"Straight ahead, Newton," called Jessica, as the big dog pulled the airship clear of the barn and into the launch area where they would begin their trip to the clouds.

"How's that?" asked Jessica, helping Newton to put on his goggles.

"Ro kay," barked Newton.

"All right," said David eagerly. "Let's get ready to drop the sandbags."

Newton dropped the sandbags one by one, and the blimp slowly rose into the air. Once they were well above the treetops, they were ready to go.

"Is everybody ready?" asked David. He flipped the fan to full speed, and the blimp leapt forward, tumbling Jessica and Newton into his lap. They flew off over the field.

"Wow!"

"Yeah!"

"Woof!"

"I don't think we should start on high speed again," laughed David.

"Yeah, next time we'll take off a little slower," agreed Jessica, as they settled back into their places.

They flew over the meadow toward the apple orchard.

"Rook, rapples,"
barked Newton.

"Steer closer so we
can pick some apples for
lunch," said Jessica.

"Okay," agreed David as he
carefully maneuvered the airship
toward the apple trees.

23

"Rook!" barked Newton.

"It's Mr. Macklebee, and it looks like he's got a whopper of a fish on his line," said David.

"Yes, and he's napping in his boat!" laughed Jessica.

"Let's go down and surprise him," suggested David.

"Rister Rackleree!" barked Newton.

"Wake up!" cried Jessica. "You have a fish on your line."

Mr. Macklebee was so startled he nearly flipped out of the boat and into the water.

The three helped Mr. Macklebee net the biggest
catch of the day.

"Thanks, kids!" Mr. Macklebee waved as they
headed off toward the clouds once again.

Away from the lake, past an eagle's nest
they rose, higher . . . and higher . . .

The airship climbed so high that the adventurers could now see all the way to the ocean. They were getting very hungry and decided to land on a nearby cloud for lunch.

After landing on the perfect cloud, David securely anchored the airship. Then they unpacked their lunch from the gondola.

"Who would have ever thought that we could have a picnic on a cloud?" laughed Jessica as she looked out over the world.

Full from their
lunch, they loaded up
and headed off once
again.

Flying down toward their homes, they neared a low-lying cloud.

"Let's plunge through it!" yelled David as he steered the airship into the middle of the cloud.

"Rall rite!" barked Newton.

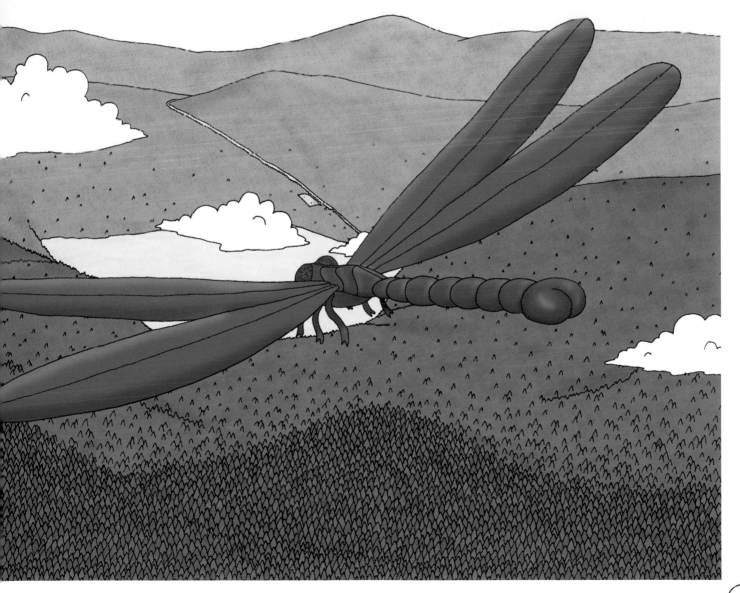

In one side they flew . . .

. . . and out the other.

As the day came to an end, the tired adventurers steered their airship home, landing gently behind the barn.

"Come on, Newton, jump out," called Jessica.
"We know you want to have more fun, but don't
worry, we'll play again tomorrow," said David.

"Rood-rye," barked Newton, wagging his tail.

"I'll meet you here tomorrow morning. How about building a greenhouse?" suggested Jessica before heading home.

"Sounds great. See you tomorrow, Jessica," said David.

"Did you have fun today?" asked David's mother as they all sat down to dinner.

"We had a great time! Dad taught us all about blimps. We built our own airship and flew all around. We even stopped and had a picnic on a cloud."

"Rup!" agreed Newton.

"What an imagination kids have. Picnic on a cloud, indeed! I wonder what they'll think up next."

Learn the history of airships and how to build your own blimp.

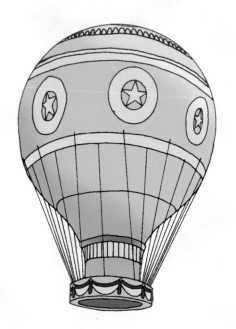

The first time a person rose into the skies was on November 21, 1783, in a hot-air balloon. It had been built by the Montgolfier brothers, who were paper makers. On December 1, just days after that first flight, people took to the skies again, this time in a rubberized silk balloon built by the Robert brothers. It was filled with a lighter-than-air gas called hydrogen.

Balloons float when we fill them with hydrogen because the gas weighs less than the surrounding air.

The next flights were in dirigibles and blimps. The first dirigible ever built was the Giffard Airship. A dirigible has a rigid frame that gives it the shape of an enormous football. A blimp is another kind of airship. It has a football shape also, but it does not have a frame. Instead, like a balloon, it uses internal pressure from the gas to hold its shape.

The Giffard Airship flew in 1852. A steam engine propelled it through the air. By the 1900s, there were many gigantic airships flying all over the world.

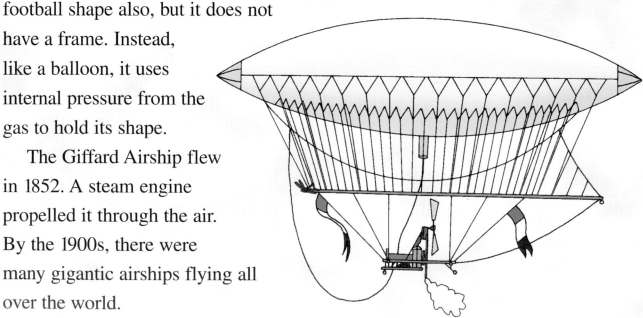

Great airships, like the Graf Zeppelin, were used very successfully to carry people and things. With some 650 flights to her credit, the Graf Zeppelin flew more than 620,000 miles and carried over 18,000 passengers!

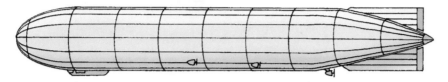

Nearly twice the size of the Graf Zeppelin was the Hindenburg, the largest airship ever built. At 804 feet long, it was almost as big as three football fields. It needed over 7 million cubic feet of hydrogen to fly! The Hindenburg burned in a terrible accident; as a result, hydrogen isn't used in airships anymore.

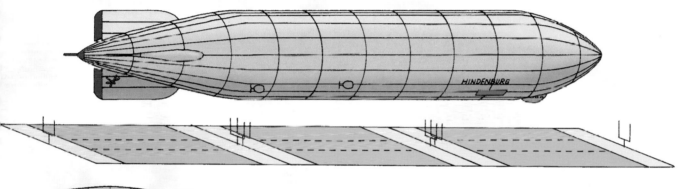

Today, we see only blimps, such as the Goodyear blimp, not dirigibles. Blimps contain a safer gas called helium and are used for advertising and sometimes for filming sports events from high above a stadium.

Maybe, in the future, we will see gigantic airships flying again. They might be used for heavy lifting or carrying cargo around the world.

To make an airship work, you need a few basic things. First, you must use a lighter-than-air gas like helium to lift the airship off the ground. Because helium weighs less than air, it floats up. (A rock, which is heavier than air, drops.) Then you need something to hold the helium so that it won't float away. Something light, like a balloon, is best. The large airships of the past used many giant, airtight bags inside the rigid frame and then covered the outside with canvas.

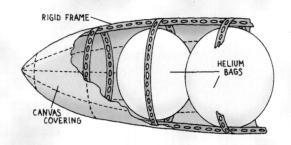

So you won't float too high, you need weights on the airship. The weights are called *ballast*. Water is used most often. When you want to rise from the ground, you drain some water out. When you want to come back to the ground, you release some helium.

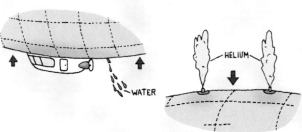

To steer to the left or right, you need flaps called *rudders*. To steer up and down, you use flaps called *elevators*. Some blimps have engines that can rotate in different directions to help steer.

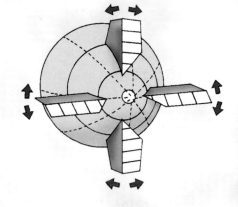

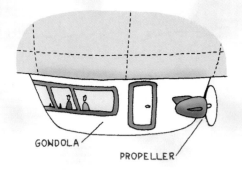

To move forward, you need a motor with propellers.

In a blimp, the cockpit is inside a *gondola*, which is like a small room at the bottom. This is where the pilot sits and controls the blimp.

YOU CAN DO IT

SUPPLIES YOU NEED:

- Thread or light string
- One drinking straw
- Scotch tape
- One pint milk carton cut in half lengthwise (after drinking the milk, maybe with chocolate chip cookies)
- Two or three helium-filled balloons (available at flower, toy, or gift shops)
- Some small toys or objects to put in the blimp

With these supplies and the help of an adult, you can have fun building the blimp below.

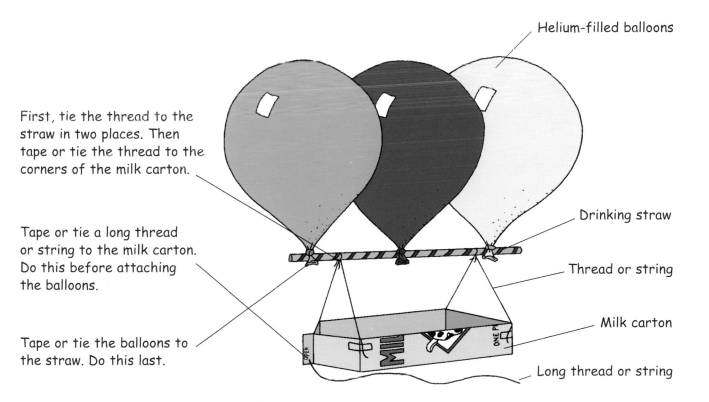

Helium-filled balloons

First, tie the thread to the straw in two places. Then tape or tie the thread to the corners of the milk carton.

Tape or tie a long thread or string to the milk carton. Do this before attaching the balloons.

Tape or tie the balloons to the straw. Do this last.

Drinking straw

Thread or string

Milk carton

Long thread or string

Once you've completed your blimp, it will tend to float to the ceiling. Pull it down with the long string. Put a variety of objects into the milk carton gondola to see what keeps it going up, what makes it go down, and what makes it float at just one height (have neutral buoyancy). Once it reaches neutral buoyancy, take the blimp to rooms or places with different temperatures. The blimp will float at different heights, depending on the temperature. This is true for real blimps as well.

You can draw people and things to cut out and put into your blimp. Have fun playing with it!